My dear Rose,

I have so much to tell you! Despite the evil schemes of the Snake, our trip to the planet of the books had a happy ending and all the books were saved!

Our journey was as instructive as it was eventful. We witnessed again how stories can enable our spirits to travel, see new perspectives, and blossom! Most importantly, however, we learned that the most beautiful stories are the ones that spring up from our own imagination. Stories like these should never be extinguished but should be shared with others.

Fox and I are full of new stories, and we can't wait to share them with you.

The Little Prince

First American edition published in 2013 by Graphic Universe™.

Le Petit Prince ™

based on the masterpiece by Antoine de Saint-Exupéry

© 2013 LPPM
An animated series based on the novel *Le Petit Prince* by Antoine de Saint-Exupéry
Developed for television by Matthieu Delaporte, Alexandre de la Patellière, and Bertrand Gatignol
Directed by Pierre-Alain Chartier

© 2013 ÉDITIONS GLÉNAT
Copyright © 2013 by Lerner Publishing Group, Inc., for the current edition

Graphic Universe™ is a trademark of Lerner Publishing Group, Inc.

Graphic Universe™
A division of Lerner Publishing Group, Inc.
241 First Avenue North
Minneapolis, MN 55401 U.S.A.

Website address : www.lernerbooks.com

Library of Congress Cataloging-in-Publication Data

Bruneau, Clotilde.
    [Planète du Ludokaa. English]
    The Planet of Ludokaa / story by Clélia Constantine ; design and illustrations by Elyum Studio ; adapted
by Clotilde Bruneau ; translated by Anne and Owen Smith. — 1st American ed.
        p.   cm. — (The little prince ; #12)
    ISBN 978-0-7613-8762-6 (lib. bdg. : alk. paper)
    ISBN 978-1-4677-1655-0 (eBook)
    I. Constantine, Clélia. II. Smith, Anne Collins, translator. III. Smith, Owen (Owen M.), translator.
IV. Saint- Exupéry, Antoine de, 1900-1944. Petit Prince. V. Elyum Studio. VI. Petit Prince (Television
program) VII. Title.
PZ7.7.B8Pj 2013
741.5'944—dc23   2013004861

Manufactured in the United States of America
1 — DP — 7/15/13

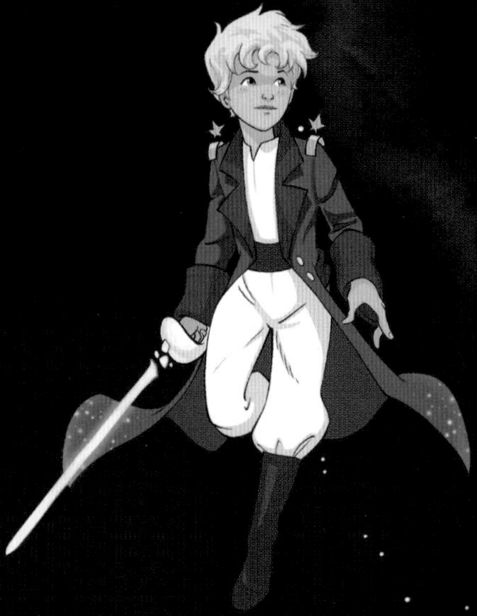

THE NEW ADVENTURES
BASED ON THE MASTERPIECE BY ANTOINE DE SAINT-EXUPÉRY

The Little Prince

THE PLANET OF LUDOKAA

Based on the animated series and an original story by Clélia Constantine

Design: Elyum Studio
Story: Clotilde Bruneau
Artistic Direction: Didier Poli
Art: Diane Fayolle
Backgrounds: Clara Karunakara-Chardavoine
Coloring: Moonsun & Laetitia Meynier
Editing: Alcino Segusa
Editorial Consultant: Didier Convard

Translation: Anne and Owen Smith

Graphic Universe™ • Minneapolis

★ THE LITTLE PRINCE

The Little Prince has extraordinary gifts. His sense of wonder allows him to discover what no one else can see. The Little Prince can communicate with all the beings in the universe, even the animals and plants. His powers grow over the course of his adventures.

The Prince's uniform:
When he transforms into the uniform of a prince, he is more agile and quick. When faced with difficult situations, the Little Prince also uses a sword that lets him sketch and bring to life anything from his imagination.

His sketchbook:
When he is not in his Prince's clothing, the Little Prince carries a sketchbook. When he blows on the pages, they take wing and form objects that he'll find very useful. Like his sword, it's powered by stardust collected on his travels.

★ FOX

A grouch, a trickster, and, so he says, interested only in his next meal, Fox is in reality the Little Prince's best friend. As such, he is always there to give him help but also just as much to help him to grow and to learn about the world.

★ THE SNAKE

Even though the Little Prince still does not know exactly why, there can be no doubt that the Snake has set his mind to plunging the entire universe into darkness! And to accomplish his goal, this malicious being is ready to use any form of deception. However, the Snake never takes action himself. He prefers to bring out the wickedness in those beings he has chosen to bite, tempting them to put their own worlds in danger.

★ THE GLOOMIES

When people who have been "bitten" by the Snake have completely destroyed their own planets, they become Gloomies, slaves to their Snake master. The Gloomies act as a group and carry out the Snake's most vile orders so he can get the better of the Little Prince!

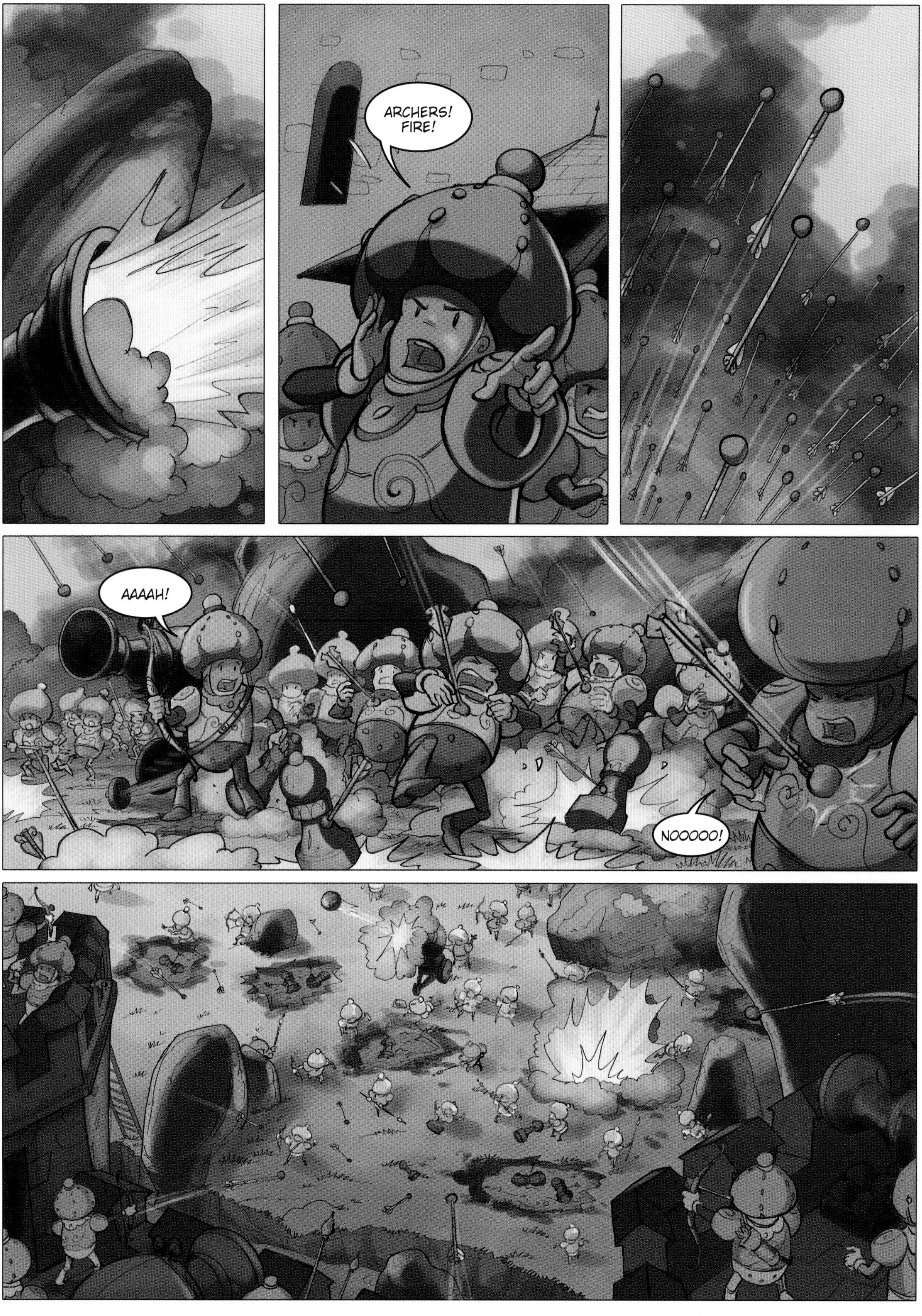
ARCHERS! FIRE!
AAAAH!
NOOOOO!

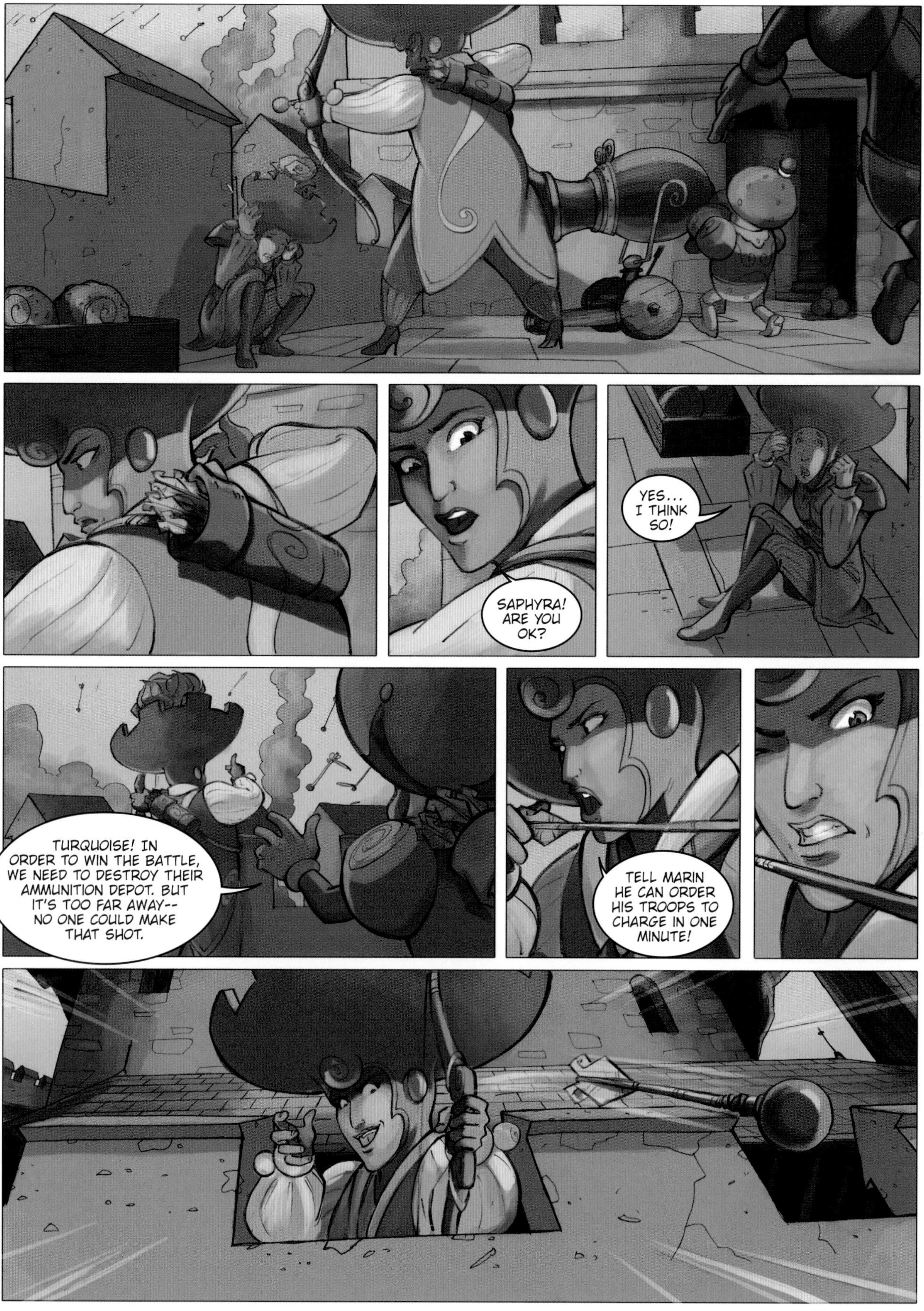
SAPHYRA! ARE YOU OK?
YES... I THINK SO!
TURQUOISE! IN ORDER TO WIN THE BATTLE, WE NEED TO DESTROY THEIR AMMUNITION DEPOT. BUT IT'S TOO FAR AWAY-- NO ONE COULD MAKE THAT SHOT.
TELL MARIN HE CAN ORDER HIS TROOPS TO CHARGE IN ONE MINUTE!

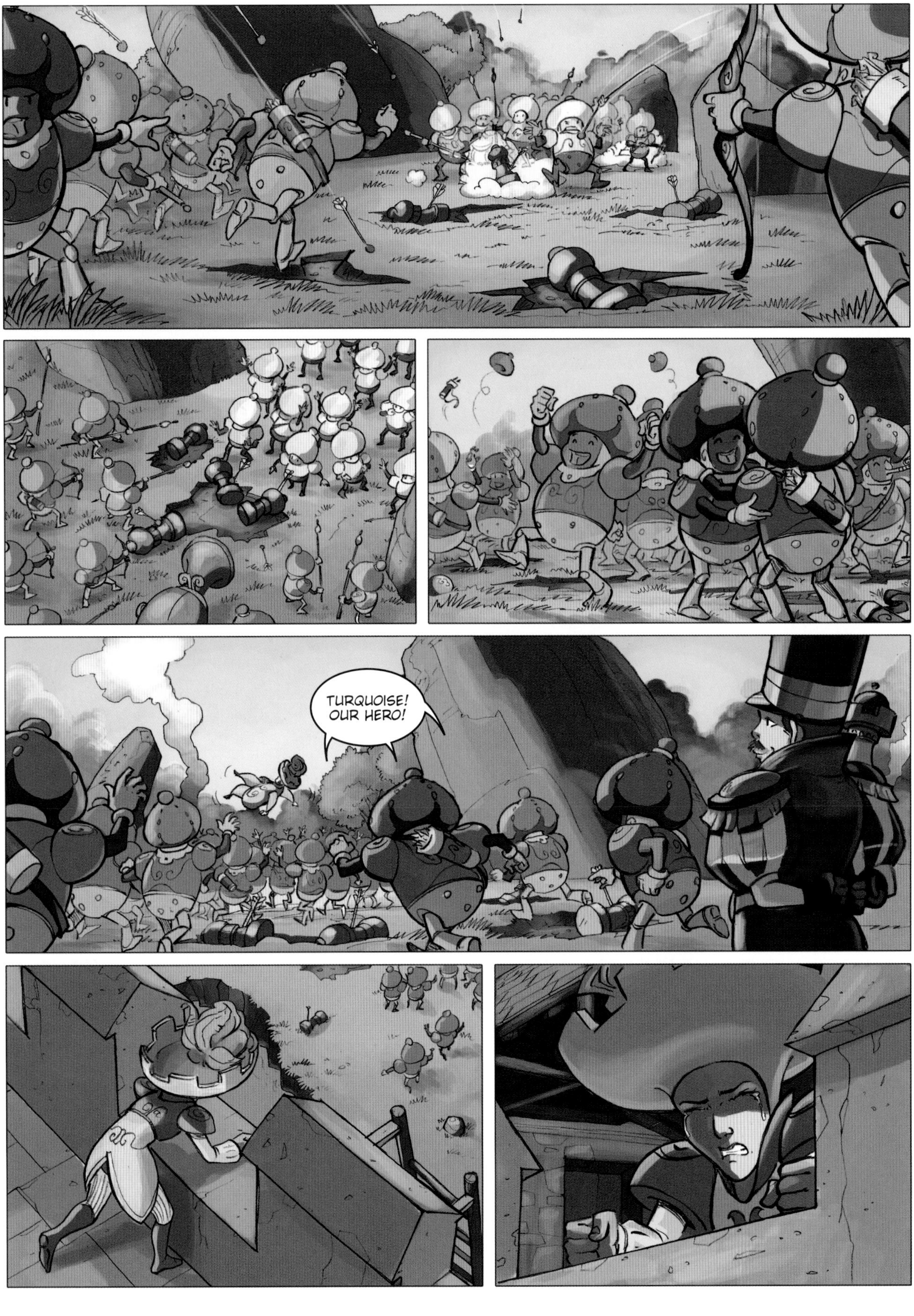
TURQUOISE! OUR HERO!

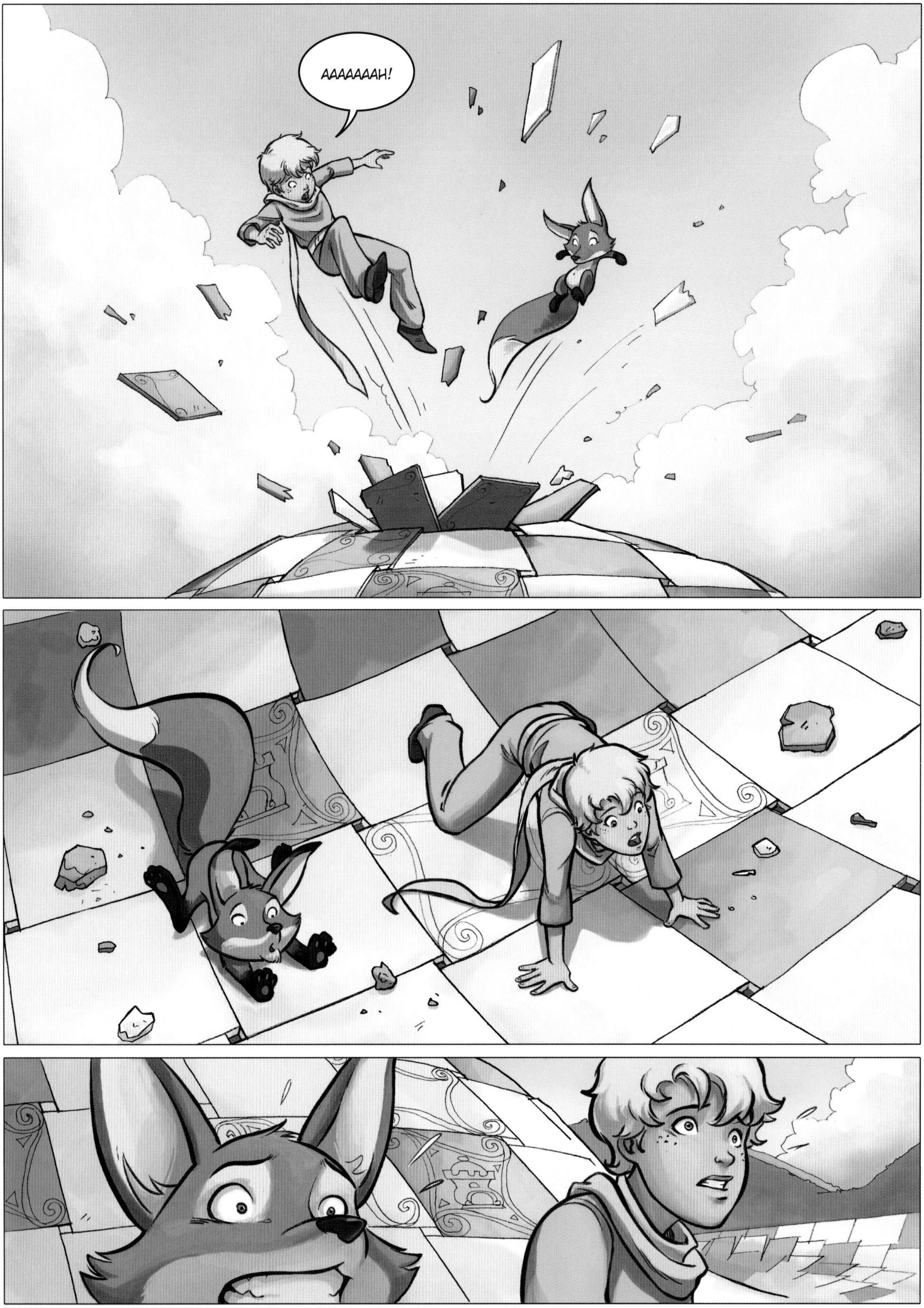
AAAAAAAH!

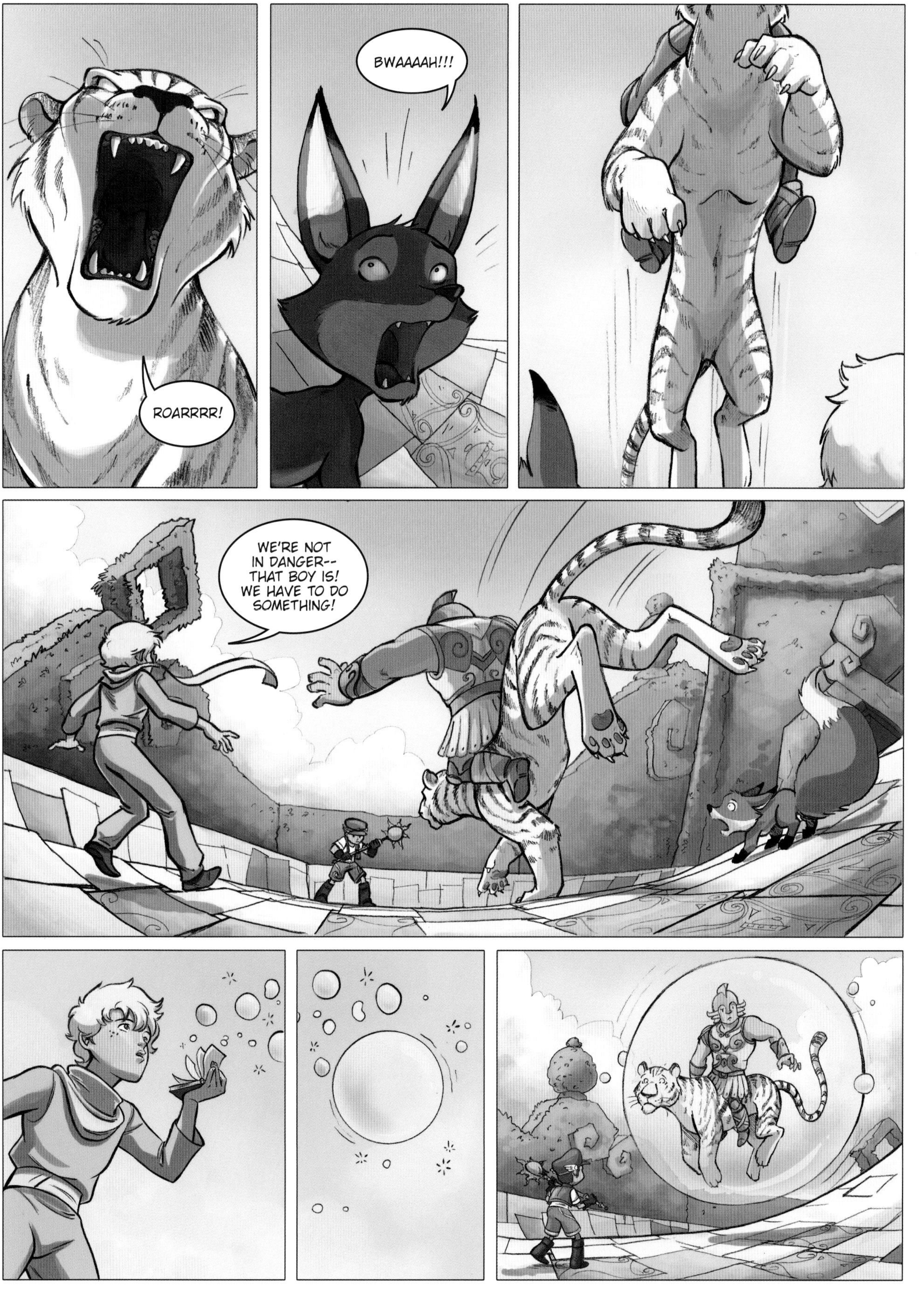
ROARRRR!
BWAAAAH!!!
WE'RE NOT IN DANGER-- THAT BOY IS! WE HAVE TO DO SOMETHING!

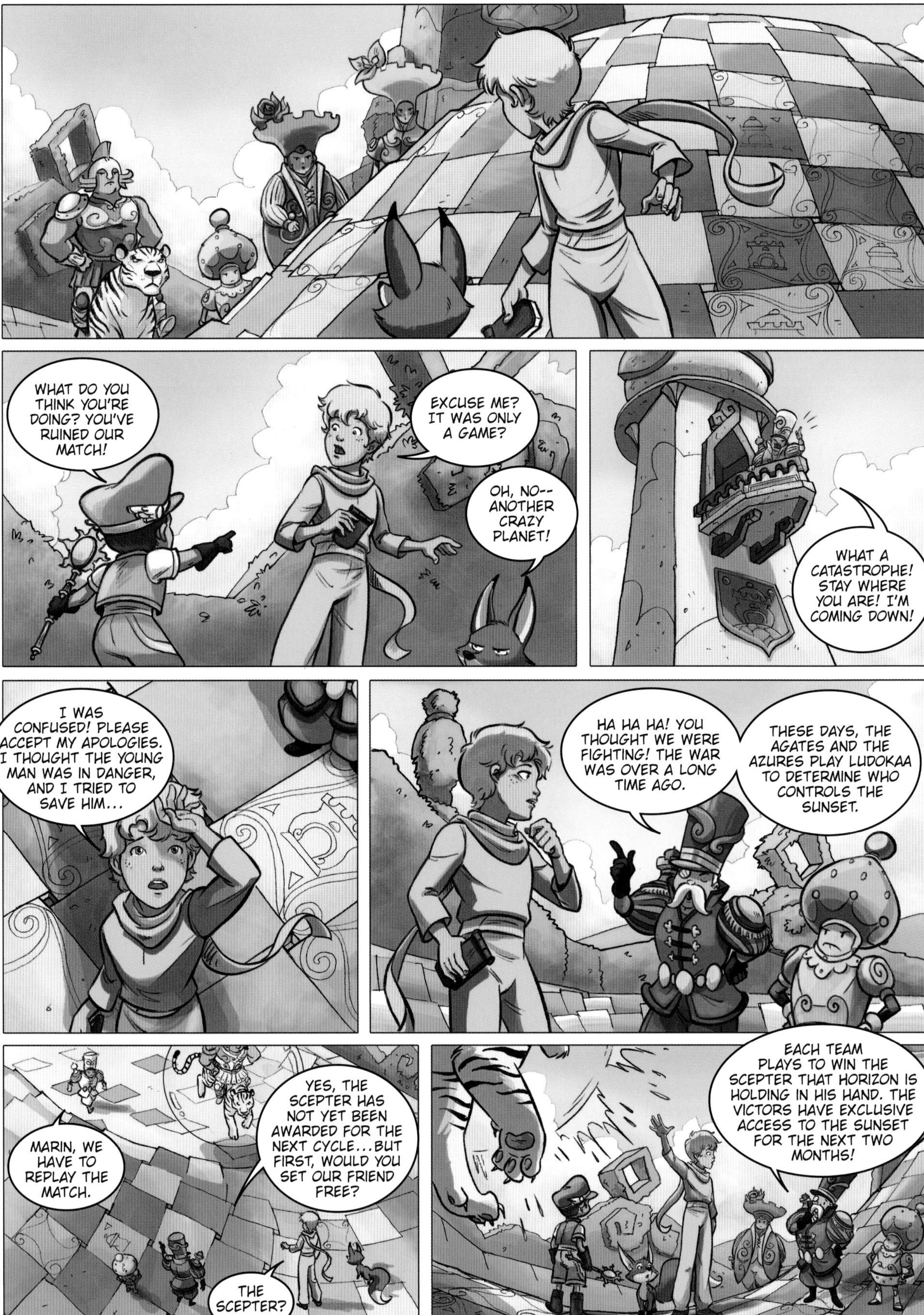
WHAT DO YOU THINK YOU'RE DOING? YOU'VE RUINED OUR MATCH!
EXCUSE ME? IT WAS ONLY A GAME?
OH, NO-- ANOTHER CRAZY PLANET!
WHAT A CATASTROPHE! STAY WHERE YOU ARE! I'M COMING DOWN!
I WAS CONFUSED! PLEASE ACCEPT MY APOLOGIES. I THOUGHT THE YOUNG MAN WAS IN DANGER, AND I TRIED TO SAVE HIM...
HA HA HA! YOU THOUGHT WE WERE FIGHTING! THE WAR WAS OVER A LONG TIME AGO.
THESE DAYS, THE AGATES AND THE AZURES PLAY LUDOKAA TO DETERMINE WHO CONTROLS THE SUNSET.
MARIN, WE HAVE TO REPLAY THE MATCH.
YES, THE SCEPTER HAS NOT YET BEEN AWARDED FOR THE NEXT CYCLE...BUT FIRST, WOULD YOU SET OUR FRIEND FREE?
THE SCEPTER?
EACH TEAM PLAYS TO WIN THE SCEPTER THAT HORIZON IS HOLDING IN HIS HAND. THE VICTORS HAVE EXCLUSIVE ACCESS TO THE SUNSET FOR THE NEXT TWO MONTHS!

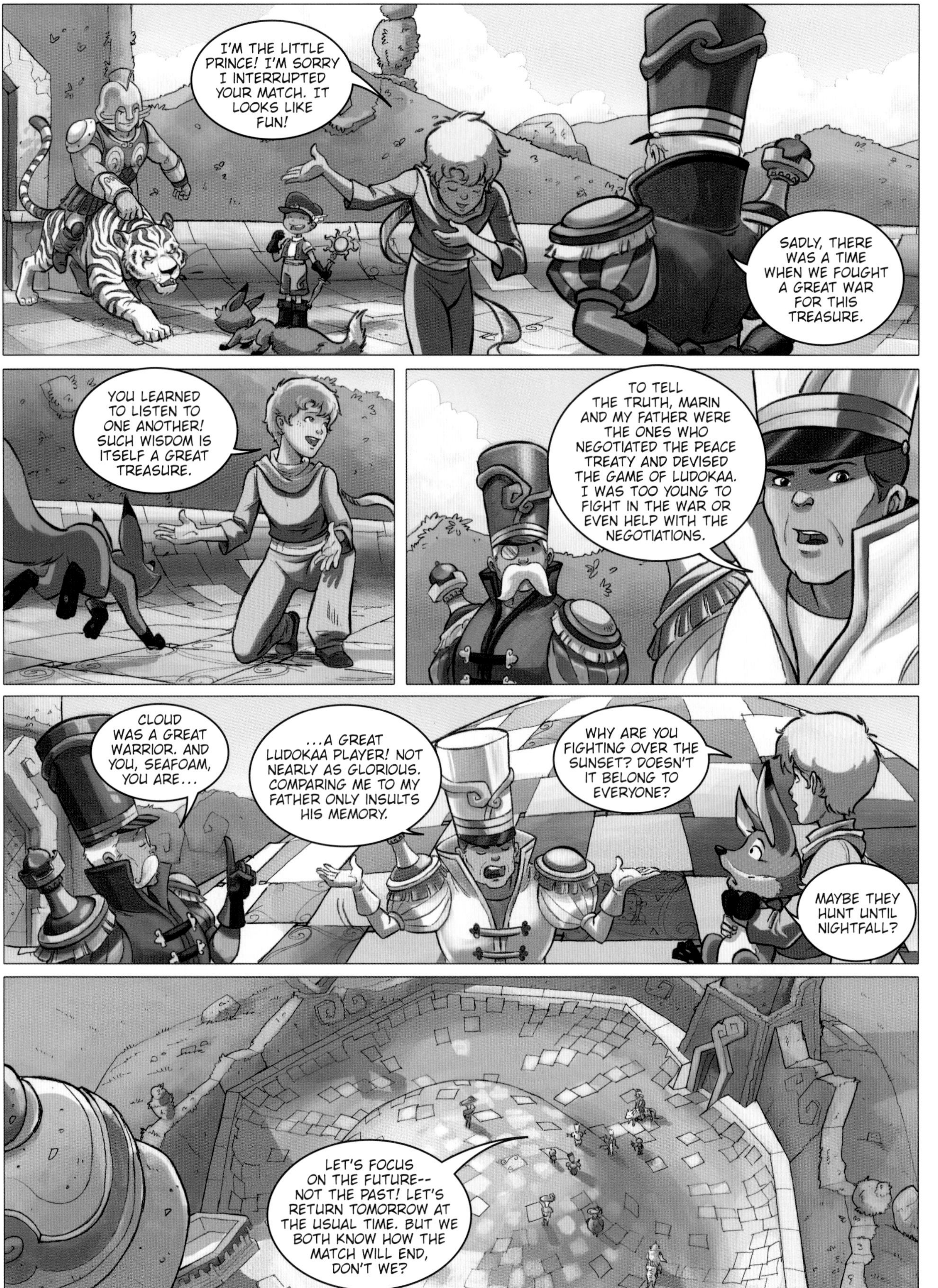
I'M THE LITTLE PRINCE! I'M SORRY I INTERRUPTED YOUR MATCH. IT LOOKS LIKE FUN!
SADLY, THERE WAS A TIME WHEN WE FOUGHT A GREAT WAR FOR THIS TREASURE.
YOU LEARNED TO LISTEN TO ONE ANOTHER! SUCH WISDOM IS ITSELF A GREAT TREASURE.
TO TELL THE TRUTH, MARIN AND MY FATHER WERE THE ONES WHO NEGOTIATED THE PEACE TREATY AND DEVISED THE GAME OF LUDOKAA. I WAS TOO YOUNG TO FIGHT IN THE WAR OR EVEN HELP WITH THE NEGOTIATIONS.
CLOUD WAS A GREAT WARRIOR. AND YOU, SEAFOAM, YOU ARE...
...A GREAT LUDOKAA PLAYER! NOT NEARLY AS GLORIOUS. COMPARING ME TO MY FATHER ONLY INSULTS HIS MEMORY.
WHY ARE YOU FIGHTING OVER THE SUNSET? DOESN'T IT BELONG TO EVERYONE?
MAYBE THEY HUNT UNTIL NIGHTFALL?
LET'S FOCUS ON THE FUTURE-- NOT THE PAST! LET'S RETURN TOMORROW AT THE USUAL TIME. BUT WE BOTH KNOW HOW THE MATCH WILL END, DON'T WE?

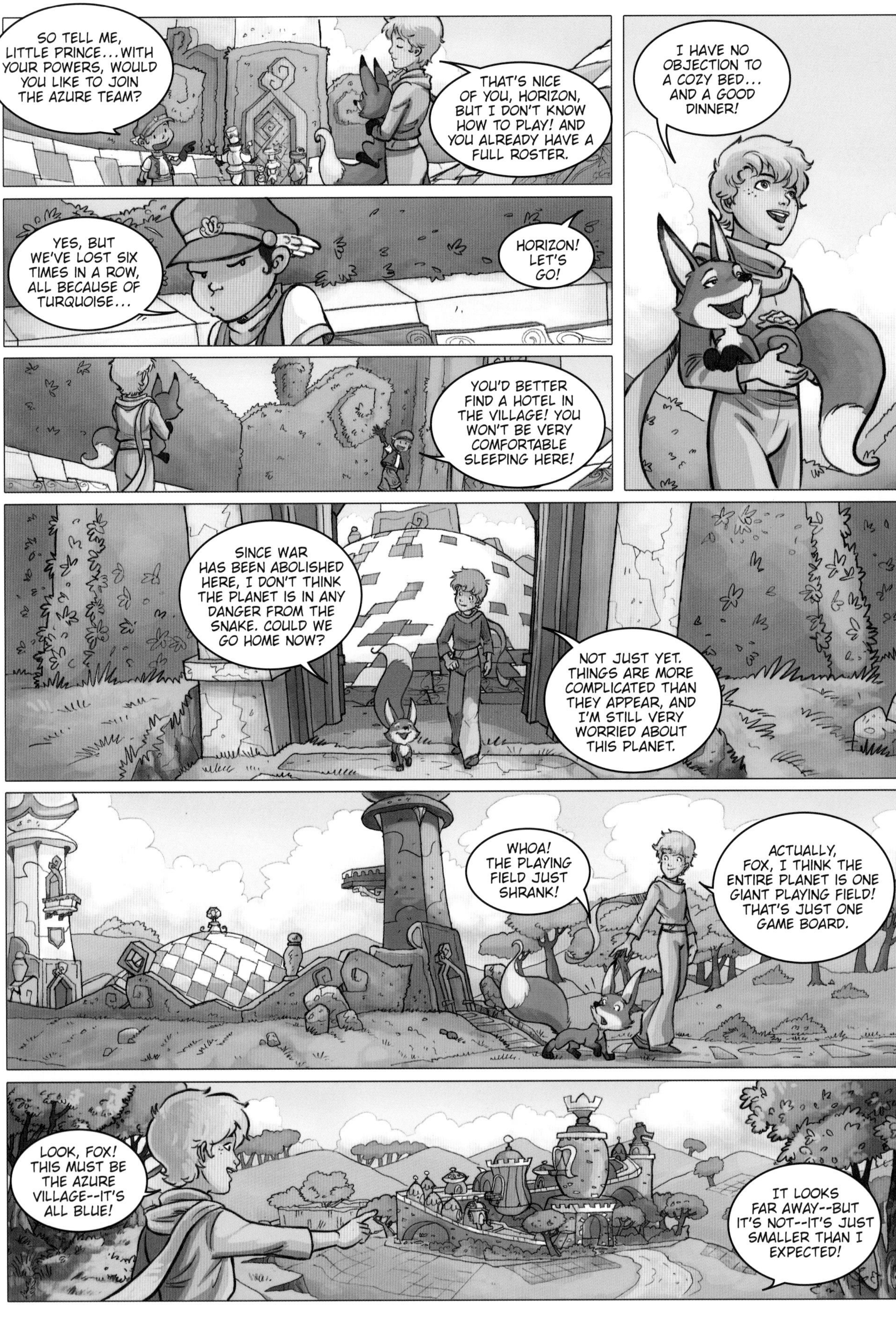
SO TELL ME, LITTLE PRINCE...WITH YOUR POWERS, WOULD YOU LIKE TO JOIN THE AZURE TEAM?
THAT'S NICE OF YOU, HORIZON, BUT I DON'T KNOW HOW TO PLAY! AND YOU ALREADY HAVE A FULL ROSTER.
YES, BUT WE'VE LOST SIX TIMES IN A ROW, ALL BECAUSE OF TURQUOISE...
HORIZON! LET'S GO!
YOU'D BETTER FIND A HOTEL IN THE VILLAGE! YOU WON'T BE VERY COMFORTABLE SLEEPING HERE!
I HAVE NO OBJECTION TO A COZY BED... AND A GOOD DINNER!
SINCE WAR HAS BEEN ABOLISHED HERE, I DON'T THINK THE PLANET IS IN ANY DANGER FROM THE SNAKE. COULD WE GO HOME NOW?
NOT JUST YET. THINGS ARE MORE COMPLICATED THAN THEY APPEAR, AND I'M STILL VERY WORRIED ABOUT THIS PLANET.
WHOA! THE PLAYING FIELD JUST SHRANK!
ACTUALLY, FOX, I THINK THE ENTIRE PLANET IS ONE GIANT PLAYING FIELD! THAT'S JUST ONE GAME BOARD.
LOOK, FOX! THIS MUST BE THE AZURE VILLAGE--IT'S ALL BLUE!
IT LOOKS FAR AWAY--BUT IT'S NOT--IT'S JUST SMALLER THAN I EXPECTED!

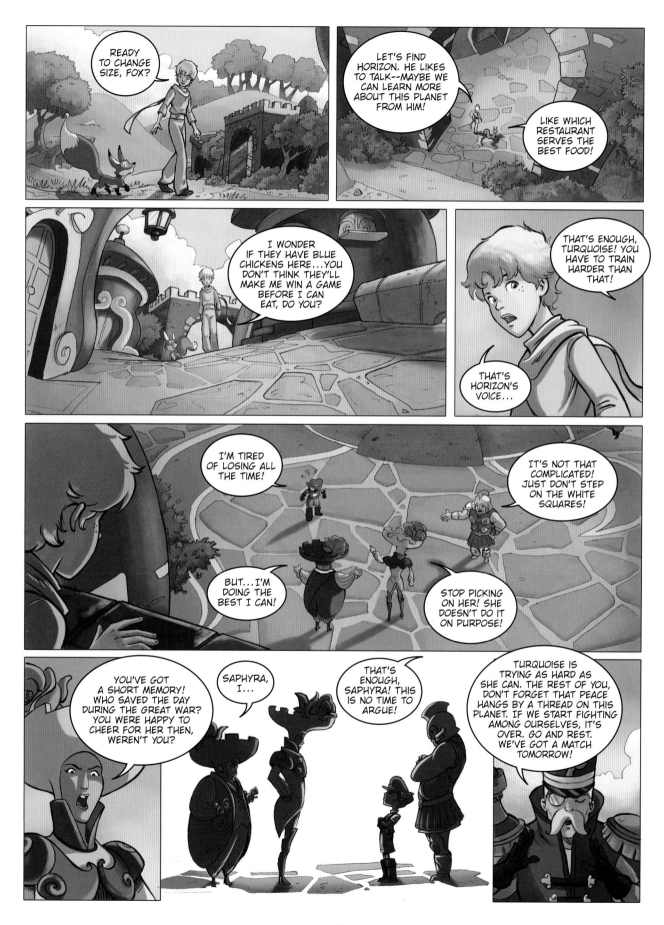

11

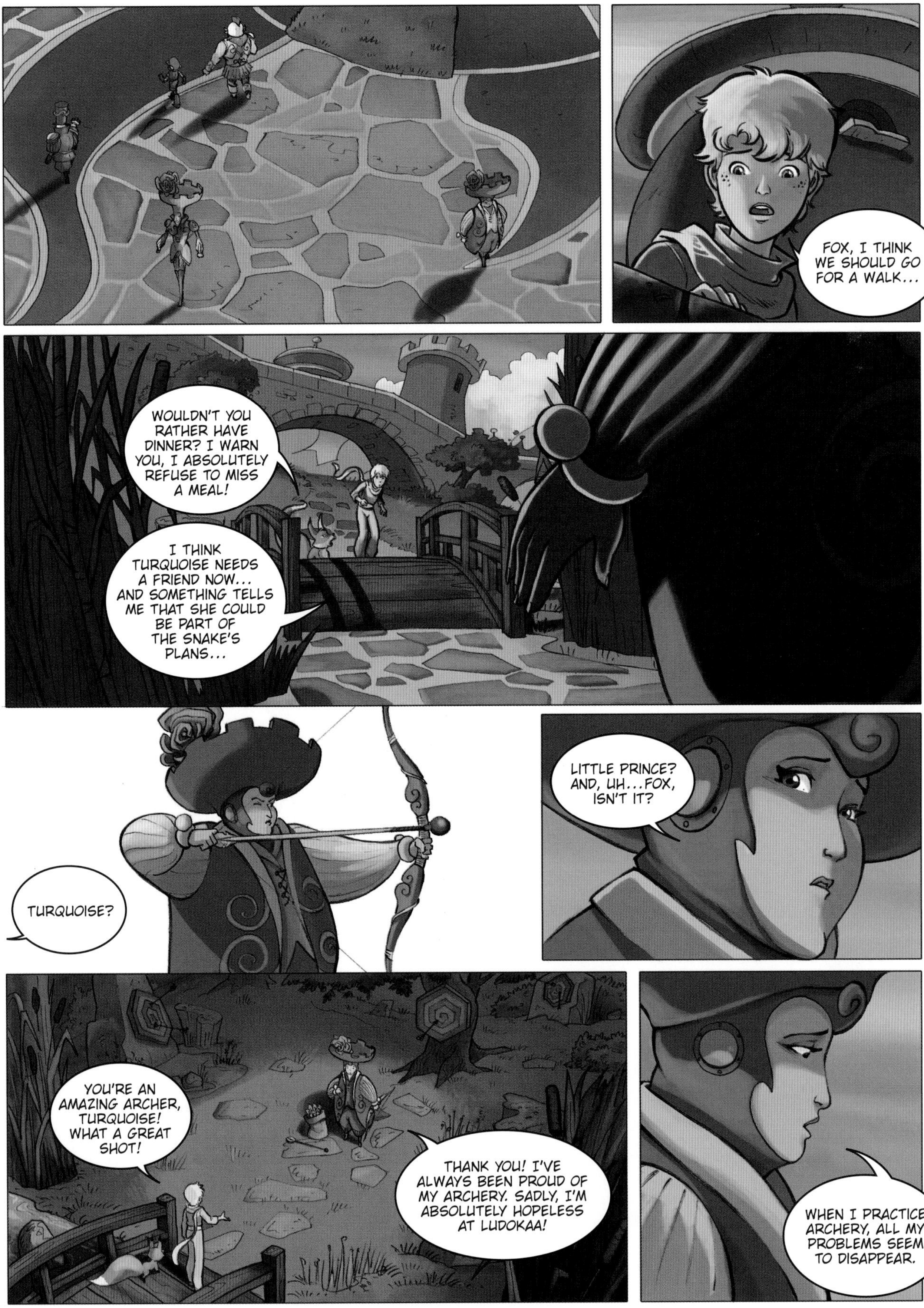
FOX, I THINK WE SHOULD GO FOR A WALK...
WOULDN'T YOU RATHER HAVE DINNER? I WARN YOU, I ABSOLUTELY REFUSE TO MISS A MEAL!
I THINK TURQUOISE NEEDS A FRIEND NOW... AND SOMETHING TELLS ME THAT SHE COULD BE PART OF THE SNAKE'S PLANS...
TURQUOISE?
LITTLE PRINCE? AND, UH...FOX, ISN'T IT?
YOU'RE AN AMAZING ARCHER, TURQUOISE! WHAT A GREAT SHOT!
THANK YOU! I'VE ALWAYS BEEN PROUD OF MY ARCHERY. SADLY, I'M ABSOLUTELY HOPELESS AT LUDOKAA!
WHEN I PRACTICE ARCHERY, ALL MY PROBLEMS SEEM TO DISAPPEAR.

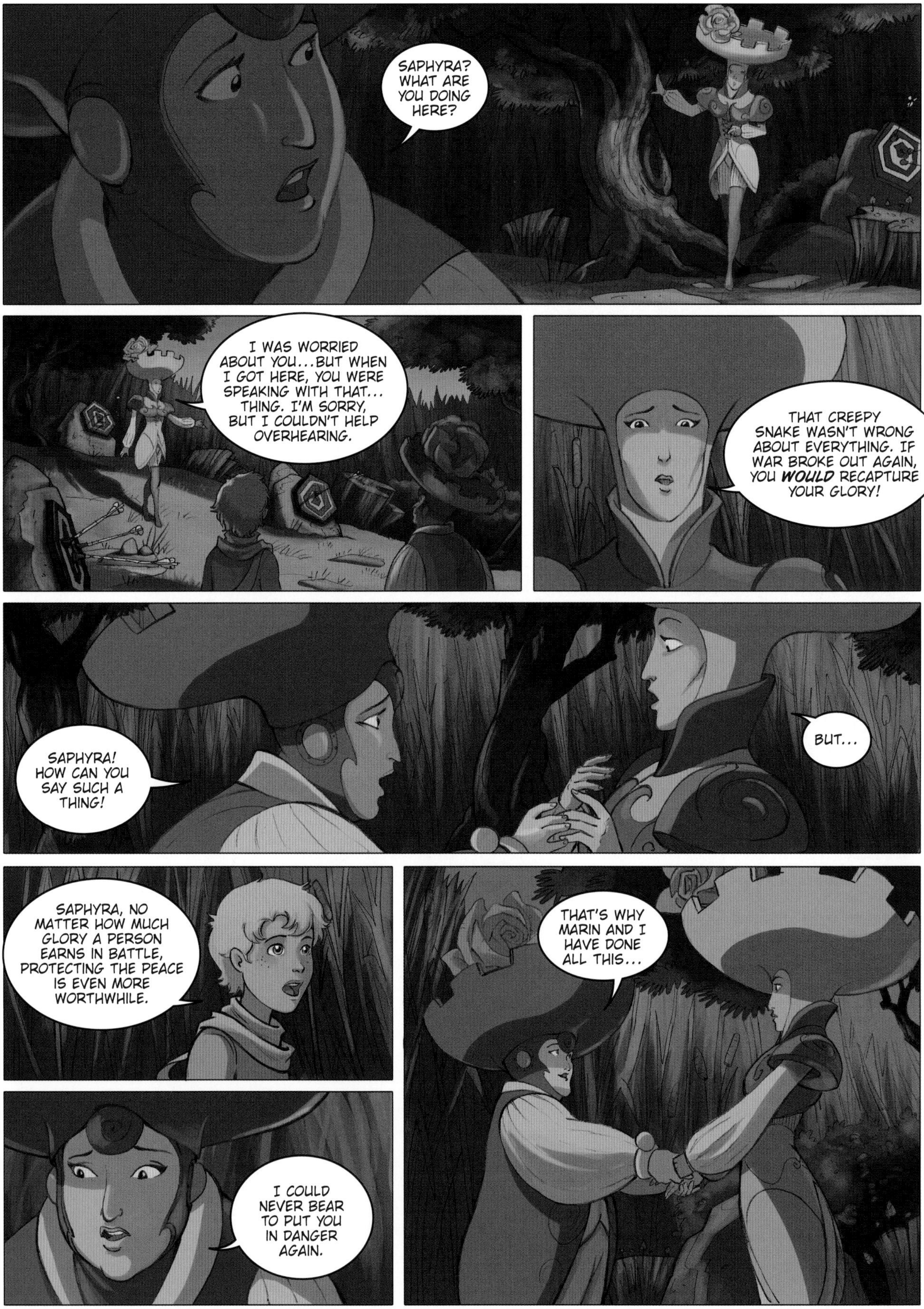

SAPHYRA? WHAT ARE YOU DOING HERE?
I WAS WORRIED ABOUT YOU...BUT WHEN I GOT HERE, YOU WERE SPEAKING WITH THAT... THING. I'M SORRY, BUT I COULDN'T HELP OVERHEARING.
THAT CREEPY SNAKE WASN'T WRONG ABOUT EVERYTHING. IF WAR BROKE OUT AGAIN, YOU ***WOULD*** RECAPTURE YOUR GLORY!
SAPHYRA! HOW CAN YOU SAY SUCH A THING!
BUT...
SAPHYRA, NO MATTER HOW MUCH GLORY A PERSON EARNS IN BATTLE, PROTECTING THE PEACE IS EVEN MORE WORTHWHILE.
I COULD NEVER BEAR TO PUT YOU IN DANGER AGAIN.
THAT'S WHY MARIN AND I HAVE DONE ALL THIS...

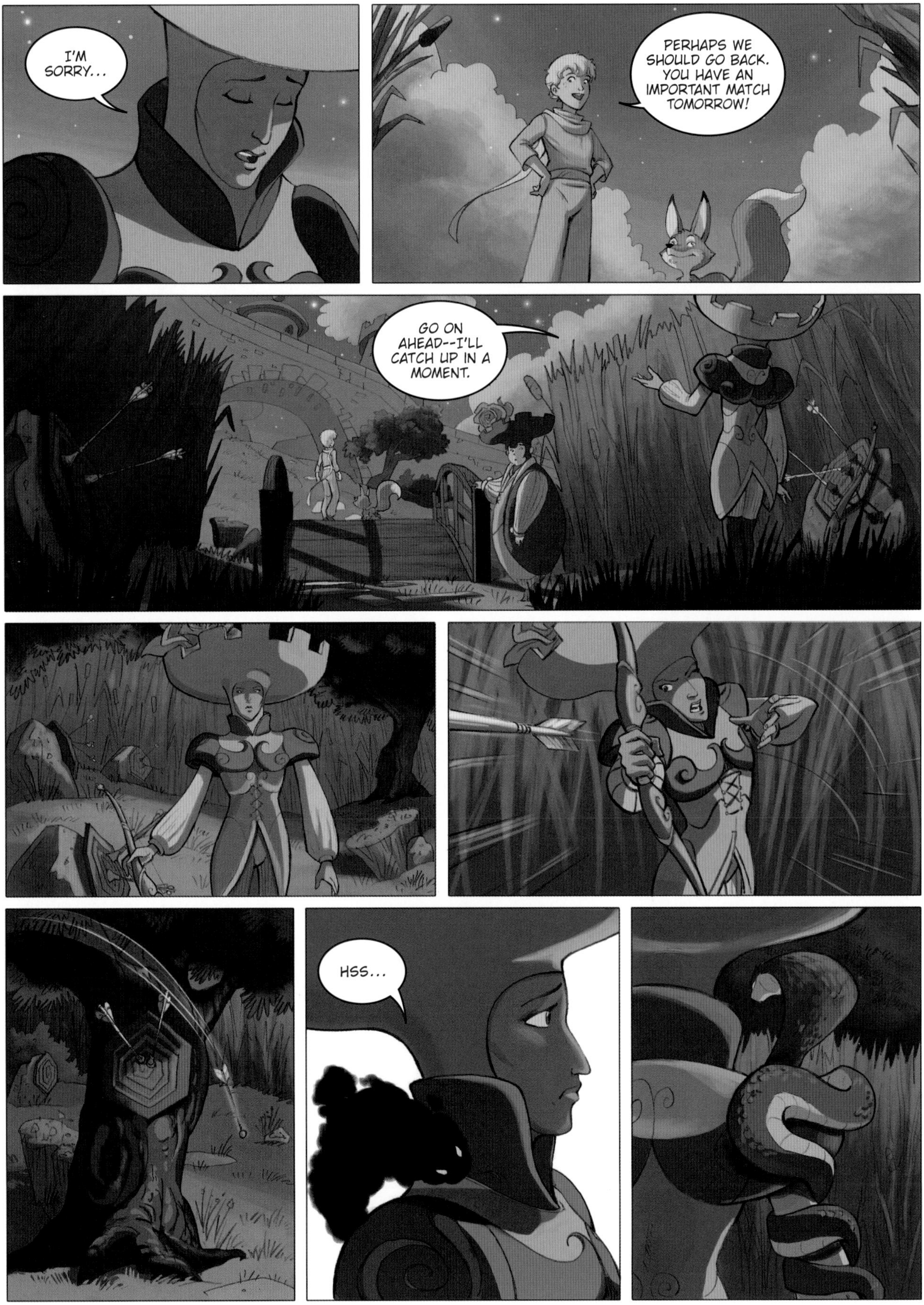
I'M SORRY...
PERHAPS WE SHOULD GO BACK. YOU HAVE AN IMPORTANT MATCH TOMORROW!
GO ON AHEAD--I'LL CATCH UP IN A MOMENT.
HSS...

17

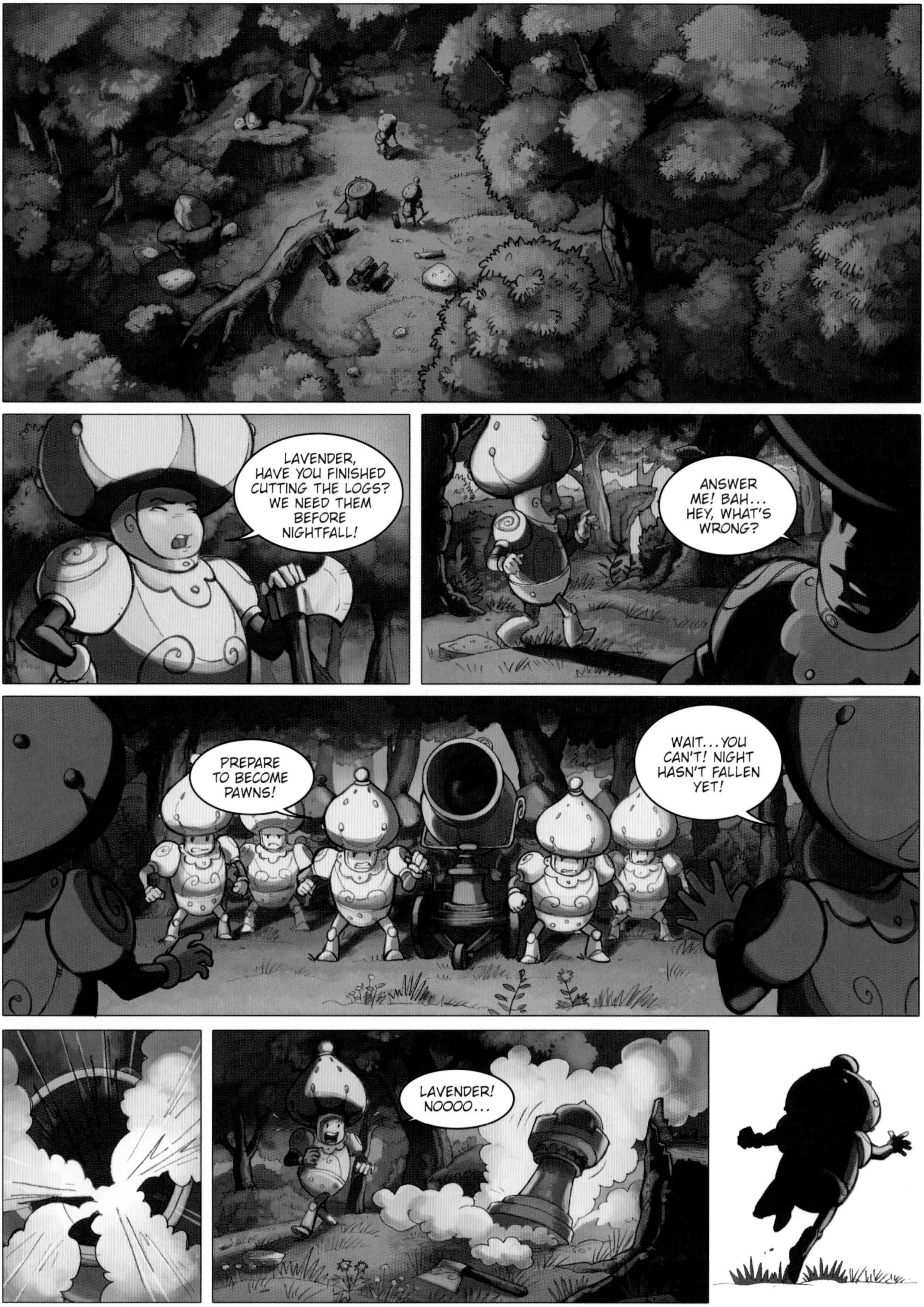
LAVENDER, HAVE YOU FINISHED CUTTING THE LOGS? WE NEED THEM BEFORE NIGHTFALL!
ANSWER ME! BAH... HEY, WHAT'S WRONG?
PREPARE TO BECOME PAWNS!
WAIT...YOU CAN'T! NIGHT HASN'T FALLEN YET!
LAVENDER! NOOOO...

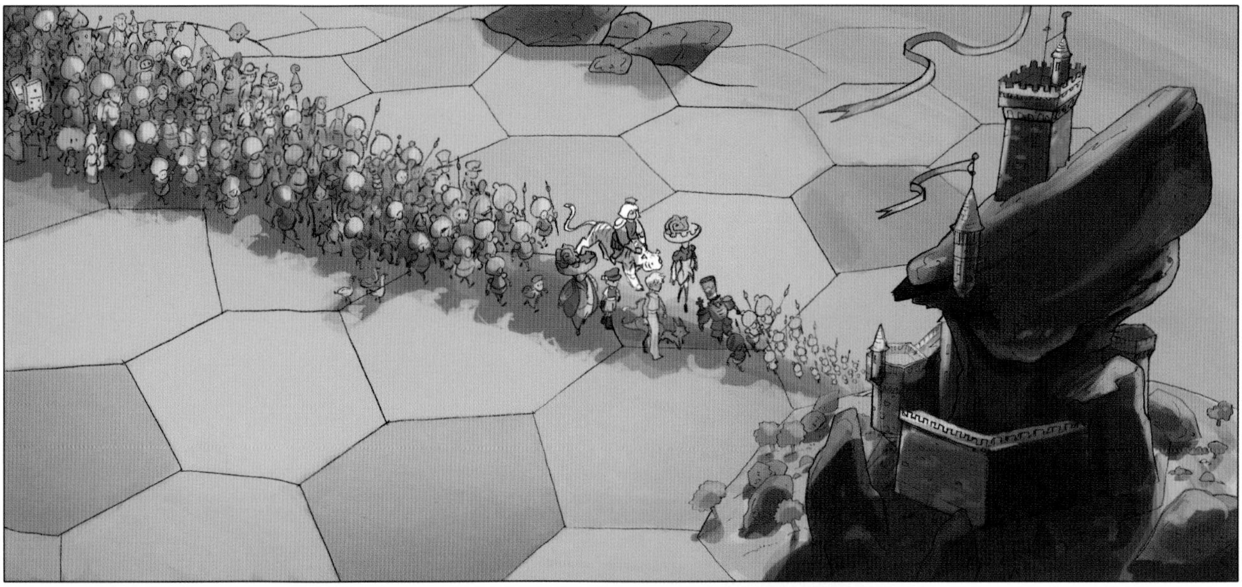

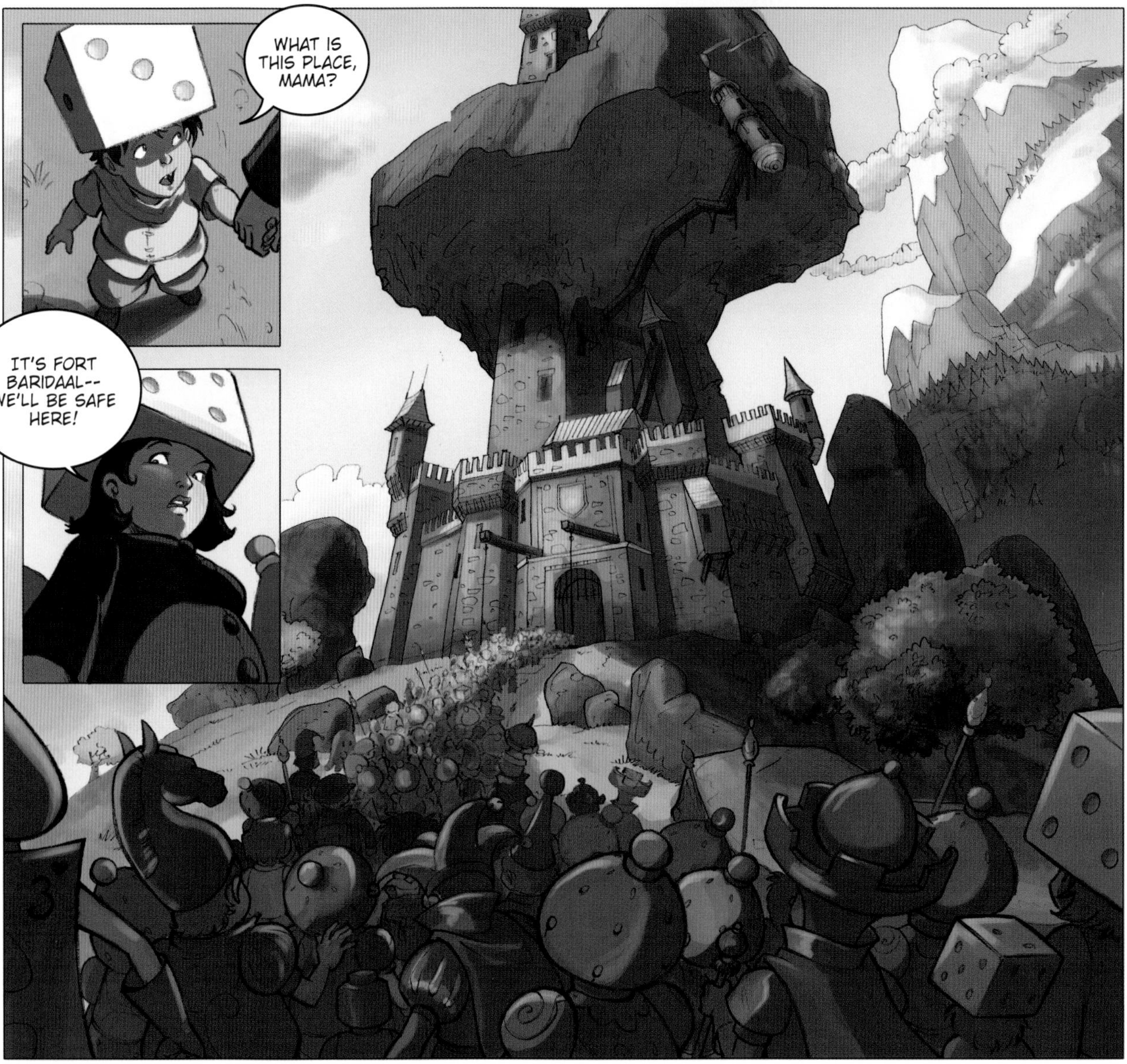
WHAT IS THIS PLACE, MAMA?
IT'S FORT BARIDAAL-- WE'LL BE SAFE HERE!

23

24

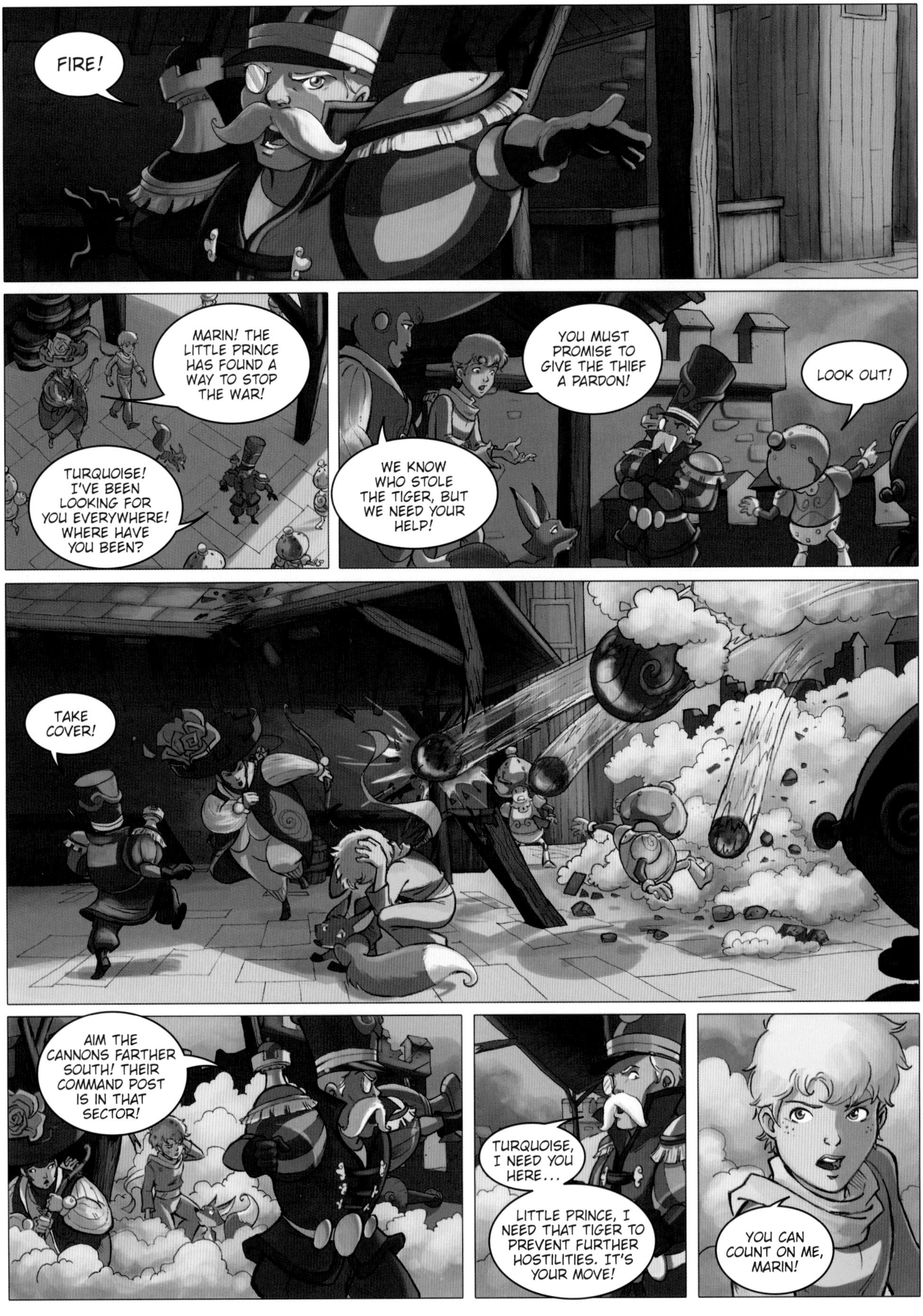
FIRE!
MARIN! THE LITTLE PRINCE HAS FOUND A WAY TO STOP THE WAR!
TURQUOISE! I'VE BEEN LOOKING FOR YOU EVERYWHERE! WHERE HAVE YOU BEEN?
YOU MUST PROMISE TO GIVE THE THIEF A PARDON!
WE KNOW WHO STOLE THE TIGER, BUT WE NEED YOUR HELP!
LOOK OUT!
TAKE COVER!
AIM THE CANNONS FARTHER SOUTH! THEIR COMMAND POST IS IN THAT SECTOR!
TURQUOISE, I NEED YOU HERE...
LITTLE PRINCE, I NEED THAT TIGER TO PREVENT FURTHER HOSTILITIES. IT'S YOUR MOVE!
YOU CAN COUNT ON ME, MARIN!

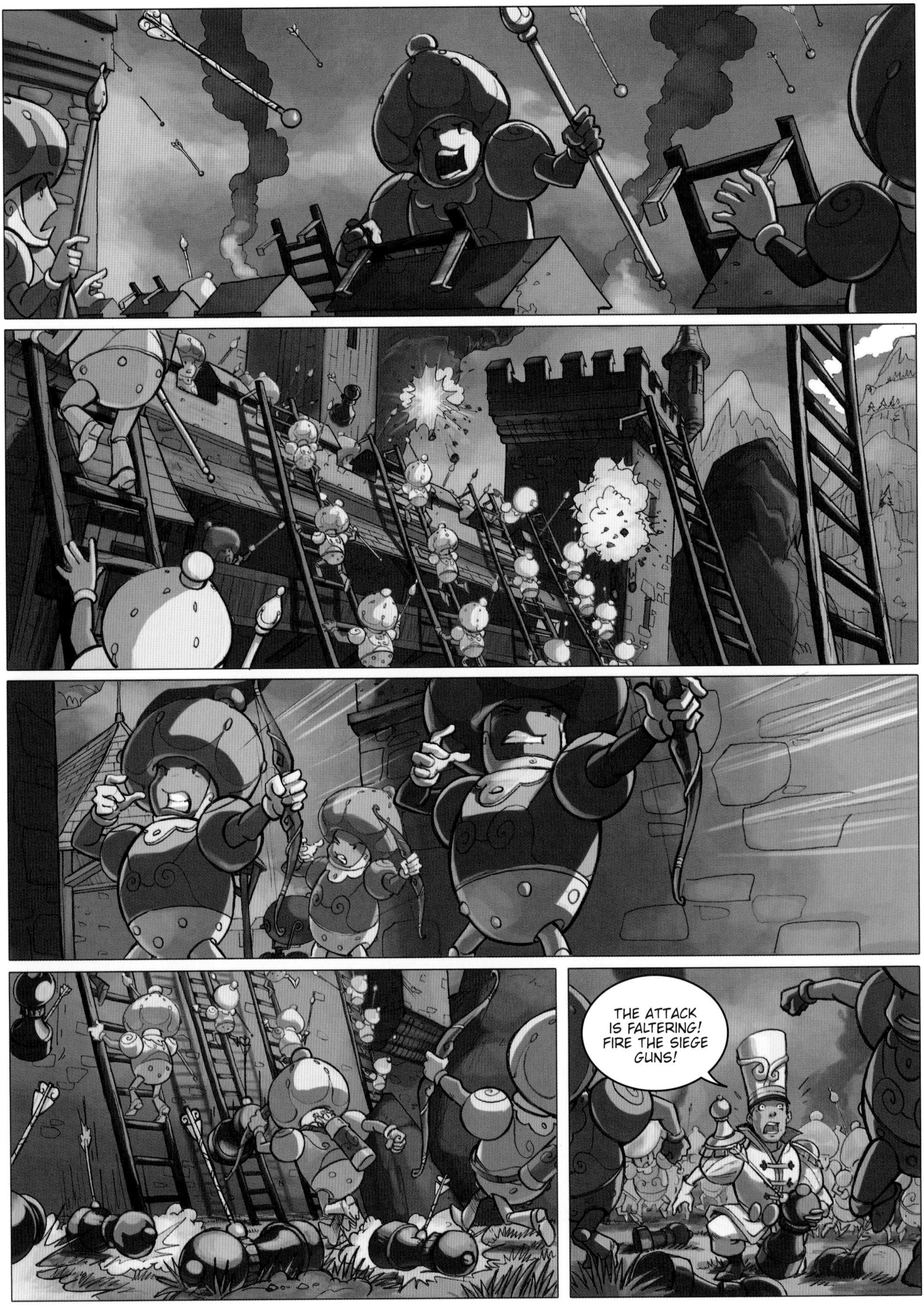
THE ATTACK IS FALTERING! FIRE THE SIEGE GUNS!

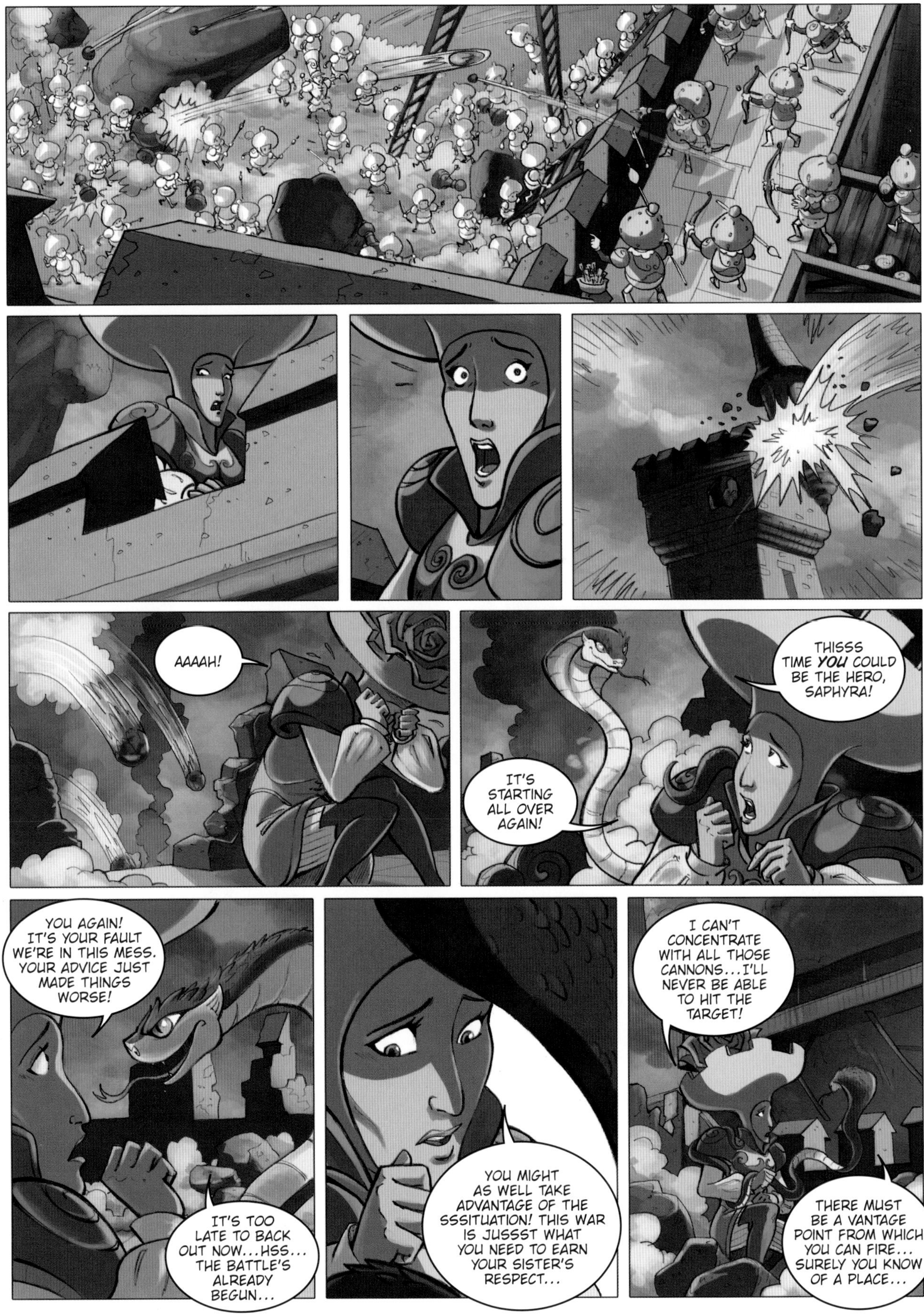
AAAAH!
THISSS TIME YOU COULD BE THE HERO, SAPHYRA!
IT'S STARTING ALL OVER AGAIN!
YOU AGAIN! IT'S YOUR FAULT WE'RE IN THIS MESS. YOUR ADVICE JUST MADE THINGS WORSE!
IT'S TOO LATE TO BACK OUT NOW...HSS... THE BATTLE'S ALREADY BEGUN...
YOU MIGHT AS WELL TAKE ADVANTAGE OF THE SSSITUATION! THIS WAR IS JUSSST WHAT YOU NEED TO EARN YOUR SISTER'S RESPECT...
I CAN'T CONCENTRATE WITH ALL THOSE CANNONS...I'LL NEVER BE ABLE TO HIT THE TARGET!
THERE MUST BE A VANTAGE POINT FROM WHICH YOU CAN FIRE... SURELY YOU KNOW OF A PLACE...

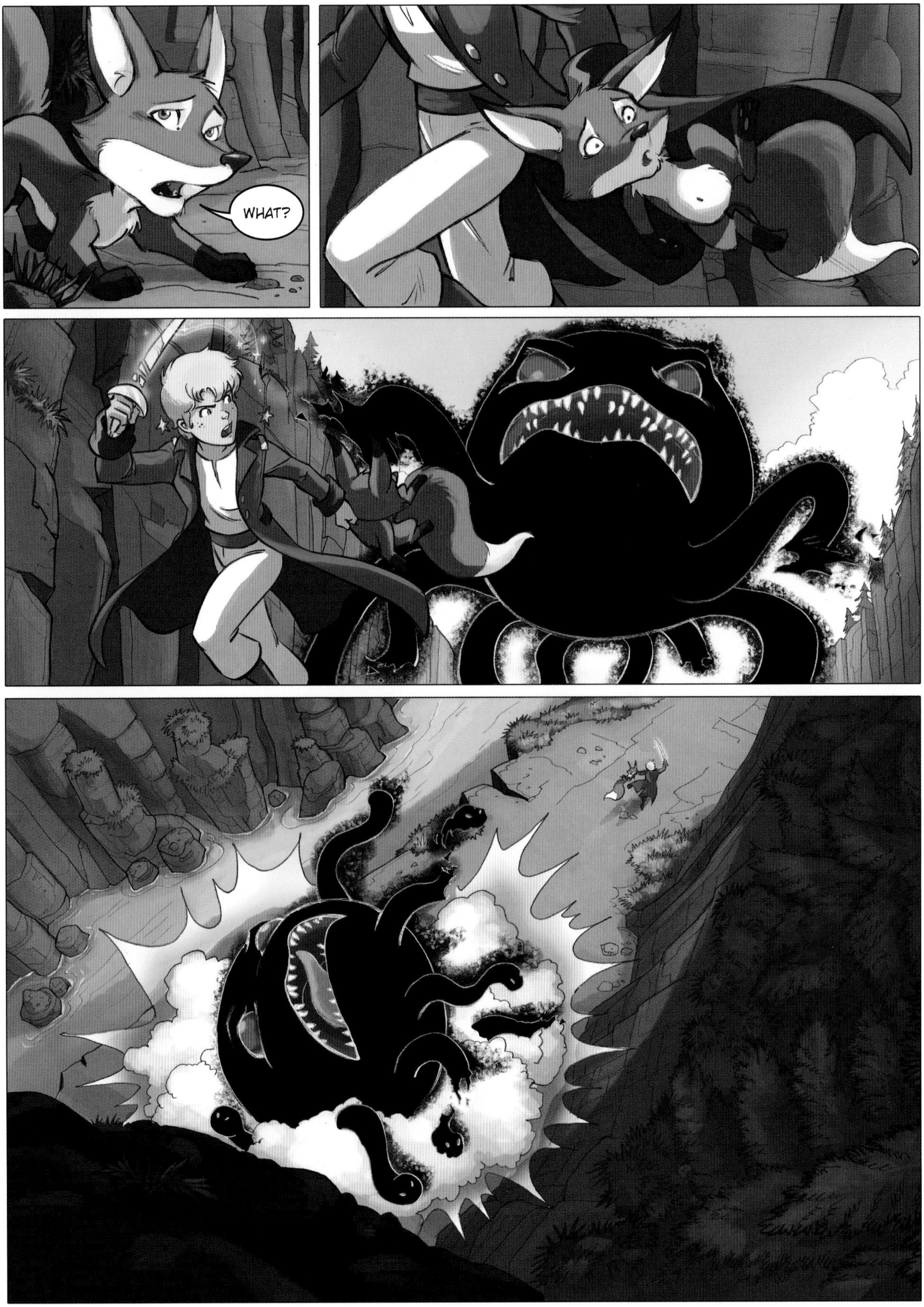
WHAT?

36

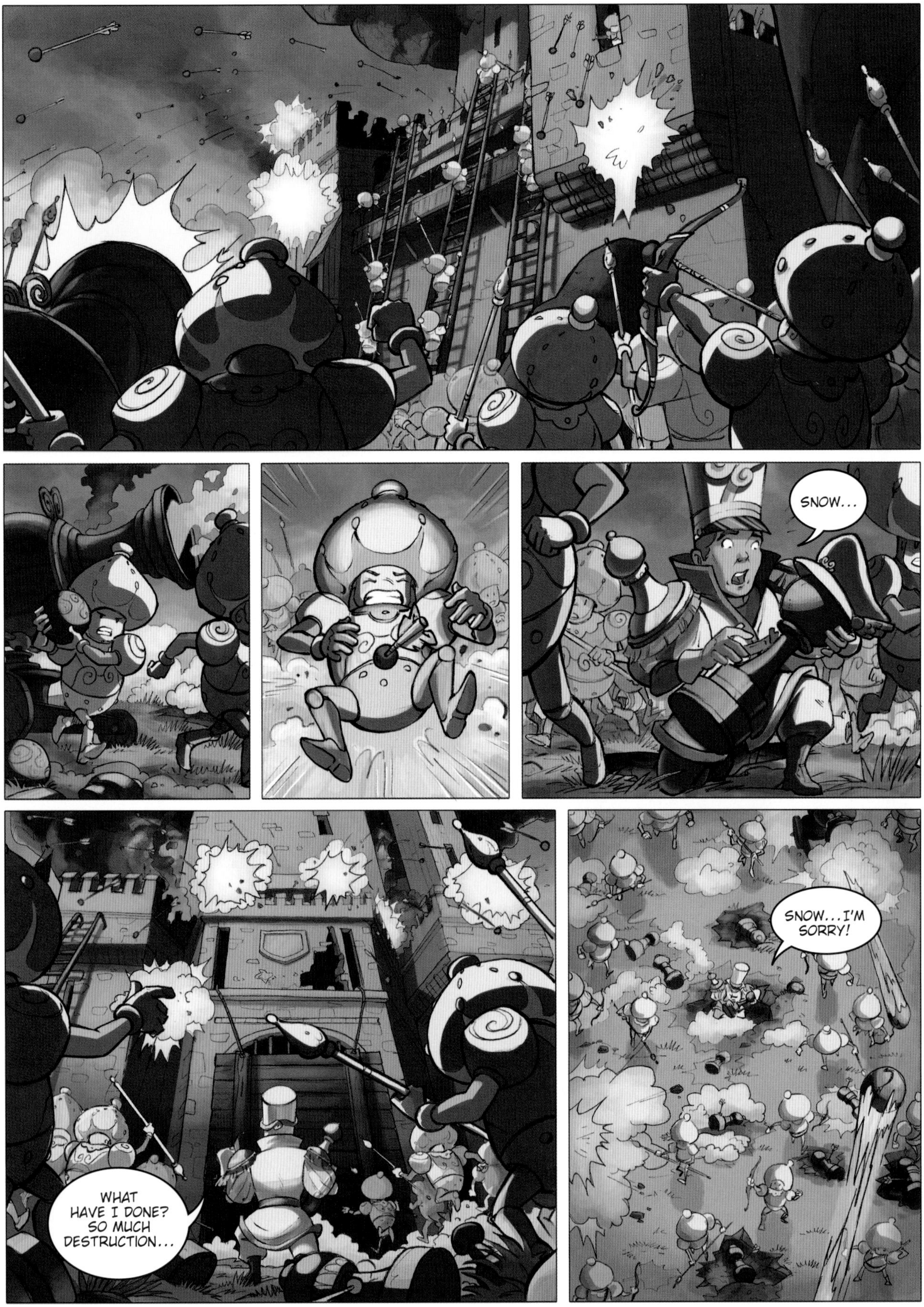
SNOW...
WHAT HAVE I DONE? SO MUCH DESTRUCTION...
SNOW...I'M SORRY!

41

43

44

THE END

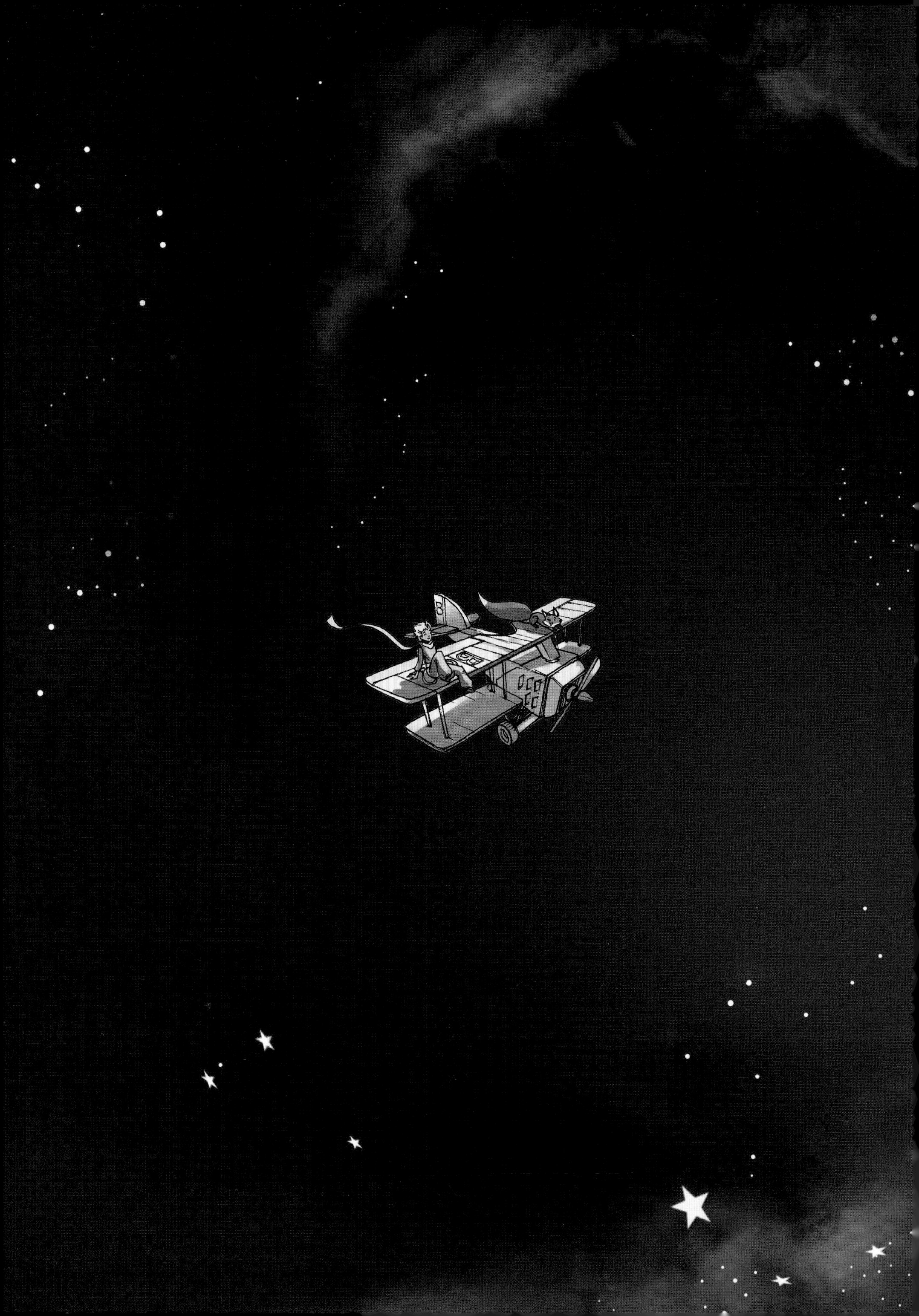
B